GLOSSARY

Aztec
Belonging to the Aztecs, an indigenous people dominant in Mexico.

Borscht *"borsch"*
A soup made with beets and usually served with sour cream.

Carnival
An annual event with colorful costumes and lively celebrations.

Cassava *"cah-sah-vah"* **Leaves**
Leaves from the cassava plant used in a tasty West African stew.

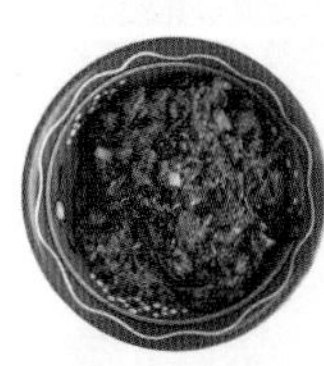

Champion
A person who fights or argues for a cause or on behalf of someone else.

Emerald
A bright green precious stone.

Glee
Great delight

Inherit
To derive a quality genetically from one's parents or ancestors.

Kinky
Having closely or tightly curled, frizzy, or wavy hair.

Lace
A fine open fabric used especially for trimming garments.

Lime
A word used in Trinidad & Tobago and the Caribbean that means "a gathering".

Locks
A contemporary way to say "dreadlocks".

Mischievous
Causing trouble in a playful way.

Mocha
Coffee made with chocolate and milk. Also used to describe deep brown skin tones.

Octet
A group of eight people or things.

Odes
Poems that address a particular subject.

Pig Latin
A made up language formed from English by rearranging syllables.

Qipao *"chee-pow"*
A high-necked, narrow-cut Chinese dress for women, made out of silk or brocade.

Pupusa *"poo-poo-sah"*
A Salvadoran dish made of a thick corn tortilla, cheese, and meat.

Realm
Land, kingdom, dominion, or nation.

Soca
Calypso music with elements of soul, originally from Trinidad.

Willful
Intentional

Wine
The name given to a popular dance in Trinidad & Tobago and the Caribbean.

Xiao Long Bao "shau long bow"
A type of steamed bun from China.

Doubles
A sandwich made with flat fried bread filled with curried chick peas.

Now, lend me your ears. There are stories to tell.
Stories of Princesses you'll get to know well.

Once there was a princess... this is how each tale starts.
So listen close to what's in the core of their hearts.

In a world that's vast; the third away from the sun.
You will find that there's a princess for everyone.

Let's tour these realms. They're oodles of fun.
We will meet each princess one by one.

Introducing Princess Ami

She is 18 years old

Favorite word in her spoken languages
Friend (English)
Ndiamo (Mende) *"dee-ah-mo"*
Padi (Krio) *"pah-dee"*

Favorite Food
Cassava *"cah-sah-vah"* **Leaves**

Learn more @ www.PrincessPlanet.com/Ami

Mauritania
Mali
Senegal
Burkina Faso
Guinea
Sierra Leone
Côte d'Ivoire
Ghana
Togo
Benin
Nigeria
Liberia

Once there was a princess full of life and grace.
She fought for unity in every place.

She had mocha skin. She had brown twisty hair.
She had gowns with lace and an African flair.

"Many hands make light work", she gave as her advice.
"If we make cake together we all eat a slice."
She led with wisdom and she wasn't hesitant.
She worked hard to become the people's president.

Introducing Princess Hui

"Hwee"

She is 19 years old

Favorite word in her spoken languages

Music (English)
Yīnyuè (Mandarin) *"ying-yeah"*

Favorite Food

Xiao long bao *"shau long bow"*

Learn more @ www.PrincessPlanet.com/Hui

Mongolia
Kyrgyzstan
Pakistan
China
Nepal
Myanmar
India
Burma
Vietnam
Bangladesh
Laos
Thailand

Once there was a princess who was cool as shade.
On her head rested a crown made of green jade.

She had shiny black hair that fell down to her waist.
She dressed in a Qipao. She had excellent taste.

She loved to find gifts from China's great past.
She shared ancient art with all who would ask.

She liked statues and paintings. She liked emerald stones.
She played keyboard and drums. She loved music of all tones.

Introducing Princess Jorjah

She is 14 years old

Favorite word in her spoken languages

Science (English)
Iencescay (Pig Latin) *"i-ense-scay"*
Le Savoir (French) *"luh sav-wahr"*

Favorite Food

Crawfish

Learn more @ www.PrincessPlanet.com/Jorjah

Oklahoma
Arkansas
Tennessee
Mississippi
Alabama
Georgia
Louisiana
Texes

Once there was a princess full of tricks and fun.
She liked setting traps and fooling everyone.
She had six brothers and a half a dozen sisters,
but she stood apart from these madams and misters.

Her locks grew long; they went down to her knees.
She wore a loose skirt. She liked shiny beads.

She loved to learn science. She followed her own road.
Science was her magic. Her potions would EXPLODE!

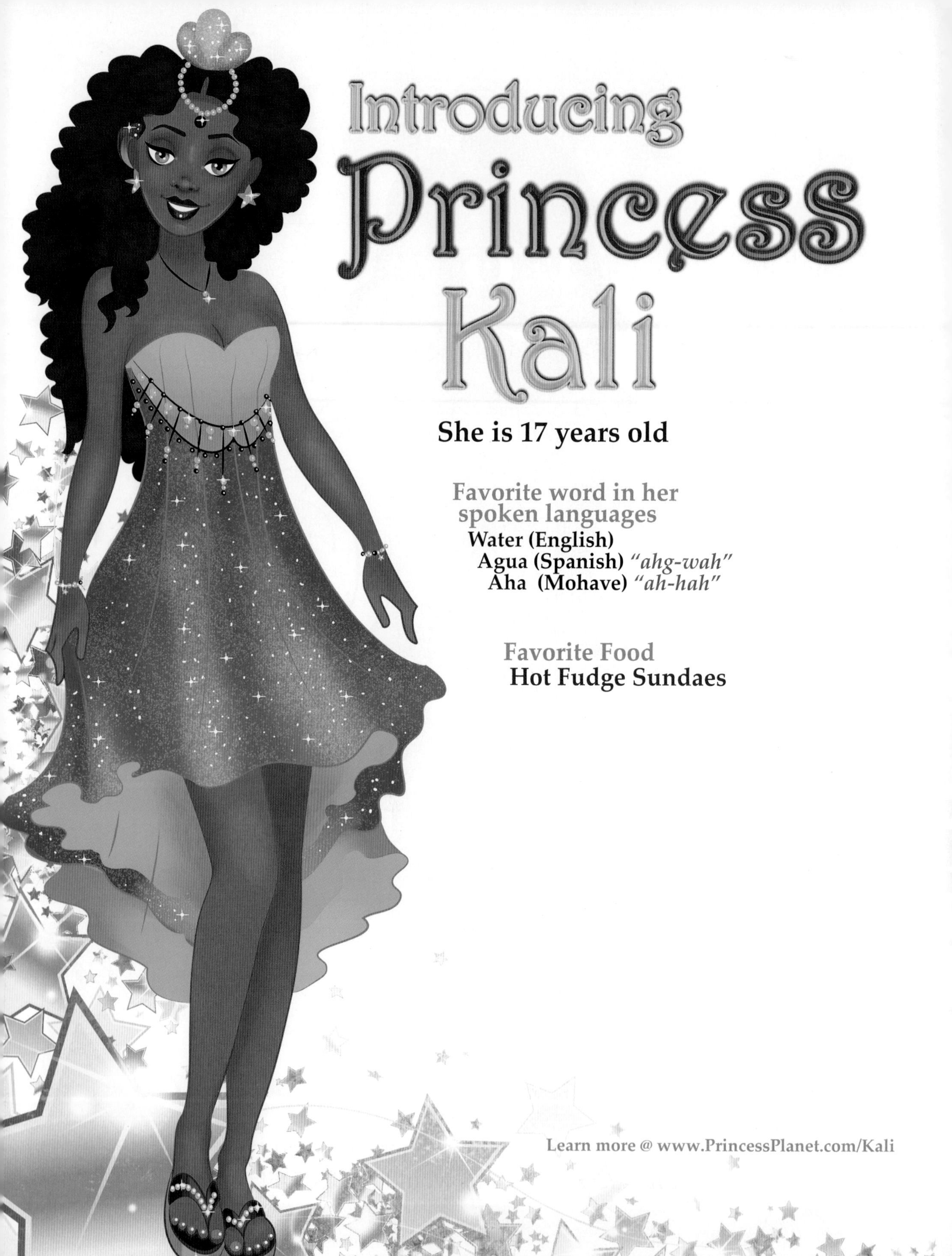

Introducing Princess Kali

She is 17 years old

Favorite word in her spoken languages

Water (English)
Agua (Spanish) *"ahg-wah"*
Aha (Mohave) *"ah-hah"*

Favorite Food

Hot Fudge Sundaes

Learn more @ www.PrincessPlanet.com/Kali

Oregon
Idaho
Wyoming
Nevada
Utah
Colorado
California
Arizona
New Mexico

Once there was a princess, so brave and full of glee.
She could walk on the land or swim under the sea.

She was willful and stubborn but giving and caring.
She watched over the sea in a manner so daring.

Her friends were a seahorse, a dolphin, and a whale.
Her legs under water would change into a tail.

Her skin was golden brown, her hair was kinky curled.
She swam with the sea life to save the ocean world.

Introducing Princess Myra

She is 16 years old

Favorite word in her spoken languages

Bread (English)

Nana (Ukrainian) *"nah-nah"*

Khleb (Russian) *"key-kleb"*

Favorite Foods

Borscht *"borsch"*

Learn more @ www.PrincessPlanet.com/Myra

Sweden
Finland
Latvia
Lithuania
Russia
Belarus
Netherlands
Poland
Germany
Czech Rep.
Ukraine
France
Austria
Moldova
Switzerland
Hungary
Romania
Italy
Bosnia
Serbia
Croatia
Bulgaria
Maced.
Albania
Greece
Turkey

Once there was a princess who cooked and taught.
She baked yummy bread and served it up hot.
She wore a gown of colors red and white.
She had a smile that could light up the night.

She wore a giant braid that hung down one side.
She liked to boil borscht. She made it with pride.

She wanted all to try. She told them, "Don't give up!"
She'd say, "Reach for the stars and win a golden cup."

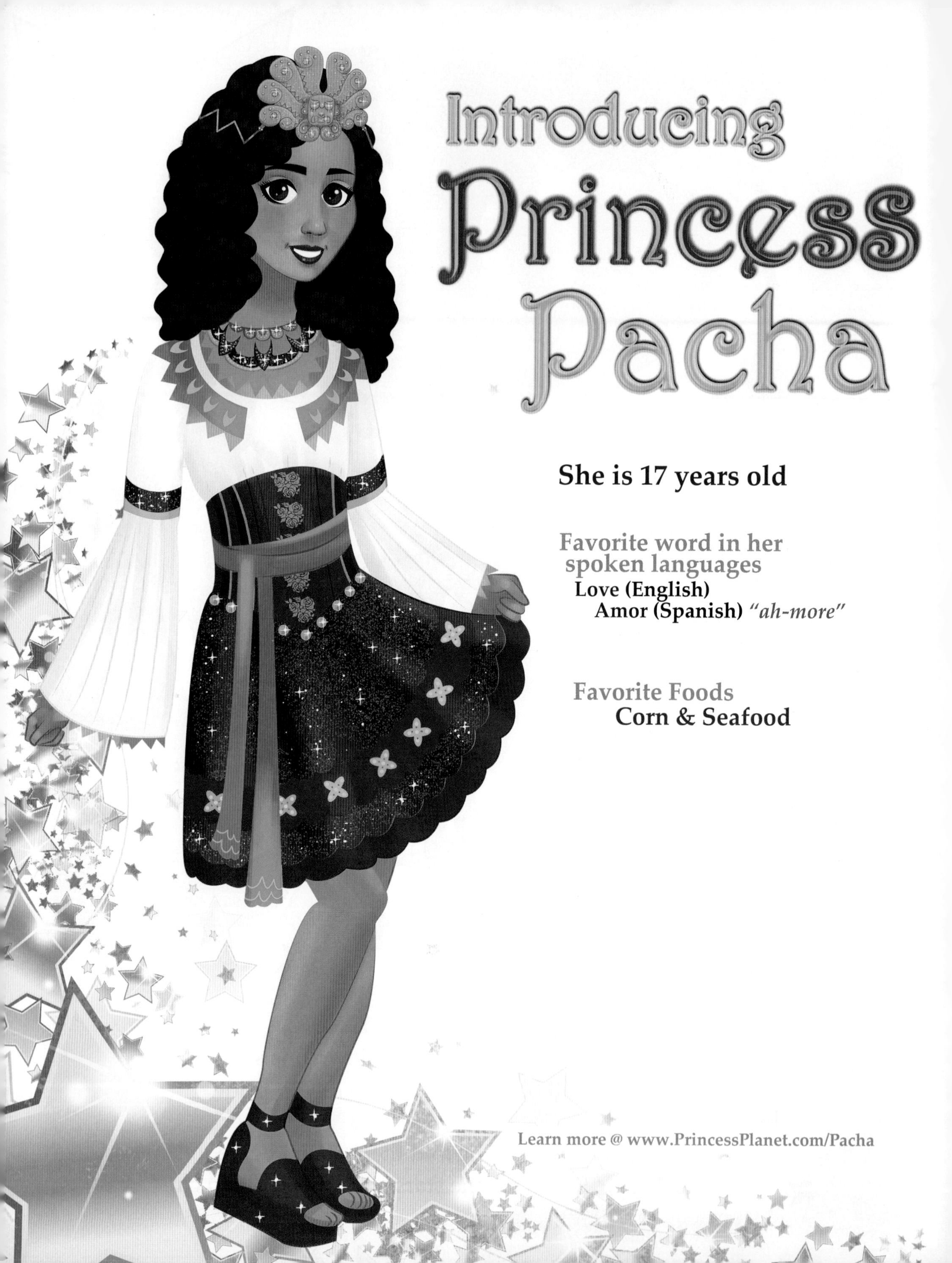

Introducing Princess Pacha

She is 17 years old

Favorite word in her spoken languages

Love (English)

Amor (Spanish) *"ah-more"*

Favorite Foods

Corn & Seafood

Learn more @ www.PrincessPlanet.com/Pacha

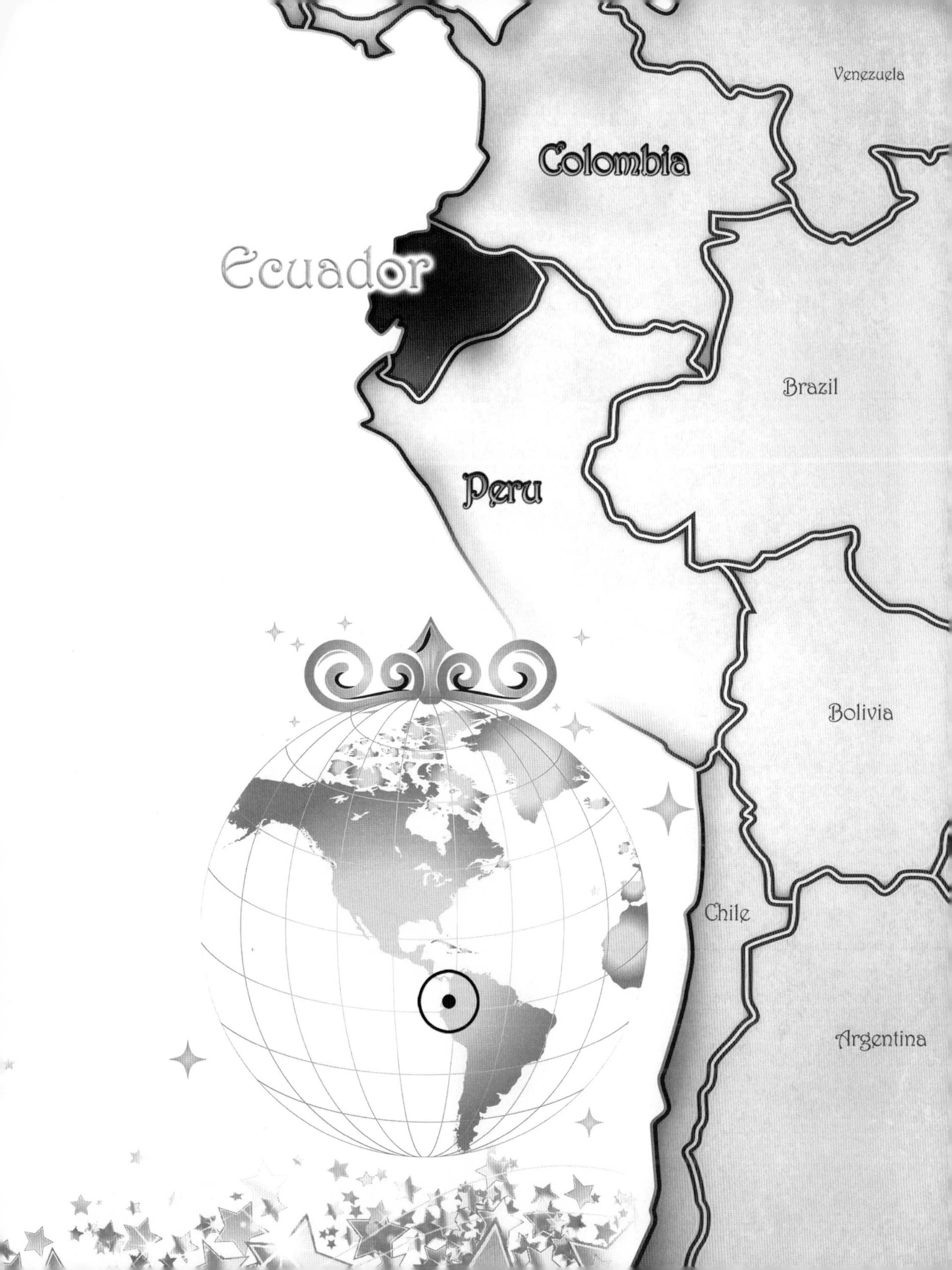
Venezuela
Colombia
Ecuador
Brazil
Peru
Bolivia
Chile
Argentina

Once there was a princess who would tickle you pink.
She wanted to learn why people think what they think.

She had curly hair that bounced when she moved.
She wore a dress that dazzled while she grooved.

She dreamed about making a perfect kingdom;
a place of happiness and complete freedom.

She had a pet guinea pig and walked with a llama.
She was polite and shy. She had excellent karma.

Introducing Princess Savannah

She is 15 years old

Favorite word in her spoken languages
Carnival (English & Spanish)
Bacchanal (Trini Patois)
"Bah-kah-nahl"

Favorite Foods
Doubles

Learn more @ www.PrincessPlanet.com/Savannah

Puerto Rico
Anguilla
Dominican Republic
Saint Kitts & Nevis
Antigua & Barbuda
Montserrat
Guadeloupe
Dominica
Martinique
Saint Lucia
St. Vincent & the Grenadines
Barbados
uba
Grenada
Curaçao
Trinadad & Tobago
Venezuela

Once there was a princess who was the life of the lime.
She would wine to Soca music at festival time.

She had curly brown hair; she had dark brown eyes.
From head to toe she wore a carnival disguise.

Nature was her love. All things green she looked over,
from growing trees of palm to patches of clover.

"Protect mother nature!" were the words she preached.
Her heart blushed for one who helped her clean the beach.

Introducing Princess Xo

"Zoe"

She is 13 years old

Favorite word in her spoken languages

Trees (English)

Cuahmeh (Nahuatl) *"kwa-meh"*

Árboles (Spanish) *"are-bow-lays"*

Favorite Foods

Pupusa *"poo-poo-sah"*

Learn more @ www.PrincessPlanet.com/Xo

Texes
Florida
Mexico
Cuba
Belize
Guatemala
Honduras
El Salvador
Nicaragua
Costa Rica
Panama
Colombia
Ecuador
Peru

Once there was a princess who was full of great strength.
When trying to save a friend she'd go to great lengths.

On her cheeks were two dimples. She never wore a frown.
On her copper toned head sat an orange and gold crown.

In the face of wrong she said firmly with great spirit,
"This land is for us. It's my clan who shall inherit".

Her native Aztec ways flowed through her veins.
She fought for her land through great pain and strain.

Though no two princesses are just alike,
each princess can reach the greatest of heights.

We are not all the same, we're unique every one.
We're all beautiful, glowing, and bright as the sun.

We hope you've discovered princesses you like.
We have many stories to share and excite.

So goodbye for now, but we'll see you soon.
There's more to come so be sure to stay tuned.

An Octet of Odes

VOLUME TWO

Daydreams Interactive LLC
If you can dream it, you can achieve it.
www.DaydreamsInteractive.com

Israel Cook - Writer, Art Director and Art Editor
Kim Archung - Editor and Co-Writer
Clair George - Lead Character Illustrator
Kafi Kareem - Copy Editor

Book Illustrations by
Clair George
Sarah Pacetti
Fifi Xu
Alif Jannata
Israel Cook
Heather Readinger

Book Layout by
Israel Cook
Sarah Pacetti
Clair George
Miriam Dwinell

Character Development by
Israel Cook
Kim Archung
Amy Beckley
Ashley Jerferson
Crystal Mckie
Kaye Evans-Lutterodt
Maria Lascano
Melisa Vargas
Xie Huixuan
Yulia Tertytsia

Special Thanks to
Ralph Cook
Sharon Wilkinson
Maria Day-Marshall
Pat Summers
Gabrielle Green

Special thanks to my Godmother Kim Archung for believing in my vision Princess Planet from day one.
-Israel Cook CEO of Daydreams Interactive

Presented By
Daydreams Interactive LLC ©

DON'T MISS...
PRINCESS PLANET
AN OCTET OF ODES
VOLUME 1
Princess
PLANET
AN OCTET OF ODES
VOL. I

DON'T MISS...
PRINCESS PLANET
COLORING BOOK
Princess
PLANET
COLORING BOOK